Child of Shadow

A Minecraft Adventure

by S.D. Stuart

Summary

Season Two – Episode 2:

Andre is captured by Shadow Warriors. Meanwhile, Larissa and Dylan continue their search for the missing Crystal Cube.

Don't miss a single episode! Be the first to know when the next book in the Minecraft Adventures series comes out. Follow the URL below to subscribe to my Book Release Bulletin for free today!

http://bit.ly/BookReleaseBulletin

Ramblin' Prose Publishing

Copyright © 2014 Steve DeWinter

www.SteveDW.com

Minecraft ® / TM & © 2009-2013 Mojang / Notch

eBook Edition

ISBN-10: 1-61978-052-6

ISBN-13: 978-1-61978-052-1

Paperback Edition

ISBN-10: 1-61978-053-4

ISBN-13: 978-1-61978-053-8

Chapter 1

Larissa landed in a crouch at the bottom of the hole dug through the floor of Dylan's prison cell and peered into the inky blackness, her eyes adjusting quickly to the darkness.

Her enhanced vision enabled her to see the edges of the roughly dug tunnel much farther than if she had been fully human.

She had the increased strength and sensory abilities of her mindless brethren, but she was a special breed.

She was not the mechanical flesh eating monster that everyone associated with zombies but a new hybrid that maintained all the intelligence and memories of the human she was before the change.

She sniffed at the air and noted two distinct smells in the tunnel beyond her own.

Dylan was not alone.

And the other smell had been the one to dig out the tunnel. His scent was thicker from the exertion of digging through the compacted soil to get to Dylan's cell.

As far as she knew, nobody in her small group was even aware that she and Dylan had been captured. So, if it was not anyone she knew, who had come to rescue Dylan?

She strained to listen for any sounds coming from the other end of the dark tunnel. Her keen ears picked up the faint scuffling sounds along with whispered comments between Dylan and someone she had never met before.

With the ease of a wild animal in its native hunting grounds, Larissa scooted forward through the tunnel. Based on the way the sound hit her ears, she estimated she would catch up with Dylan in less than a few minutes.

She dashed forward on all fours until she came to another hole that had led straight down. She couldn't see the other end of this crudely carved tunnel, but the sounds and smells of Dylan were definitely coming from this new hole.

She dropped over the edge of the hole and, pressing her feet and hands against the sides, lowered herself slowly until she reached a new cross tunnel at the bottom that stretched on for miles in both directions.

She followed Dylan's smell until she came to a grate in the wall that had been pulled away and left open.

She moved forward to the edge of the opening and peeked around the edge. The room beyond was lit by flaming torches mounted on the wall.

Dylan and the unknown man, judging by his smell, were both tied up to the same pillar in the middle of the room.

They stood side by side, their arms raised above their heads and chained to the ceiling. It seemed overkill to chain them to the ceiling and tie them to the center post.

She sniffed at the air, but could not find a trace of anyone else with them.

As far as all her senses could detect, the two men tied to the support beam were alone. They certainly would not have tied themselves up. So, where were the scents of the others who had captured them?

She leaned farther through the grate to see into the rest of the room and froze.

She could neither see, nor smell, nor hear the group of hooded figures whose shadows were cast along the walls of the room. The room was empty except for the shadows that started on the ground and stretched and flickered in the dancing torchlight.

Judging by the angles of the shadows, it appeared a large group of hooded figures were facing both Dylan and the man with him.

They looked like they were chanting and swaying in time to some unheard rhythm but the only thing she could hear was Dylan and his new companion whispering to each other about the unnerving silence from their invisible captors.

She started to lean back out of sight when something caught her eye and she paused. Down along the same wall she was against sat a large cauldron. The steam rising from it telegraphed that the contents inside was either boiling hot or close to boiling.

As she leaned against the wall it crumbled wetly in her hand and broke away easily. She grinned to herself as an idea formed in her mind.

She slowly backed out through the open grate and looked along the tunnel that stretched to infinity.

Light spilled into the hallway in sharp angles at evenly spaced intervals indicating that there were additional tunnels that intersected this one.

The tunnel she was in stretched for so long, it might travel under the entire castle and beyond, maybe even to the next town. It was so long and straight, it might even lead all the way to the portal that would take her out of this realm and into the creator's world.

But before she could do that, she had to find the Crystal Cube that activated the portal. And Dylan was the only one who knew where it might be.

So she had to rescue him first.

She headed down the tunnel, pacing out the length in her mind until she was certain she was at the same spot as the cauldron but on the other side of the wall.

She dug her hand into the wet earth and scooped away a large chunk of the wall. She grabbed more mud with her other hand, getting into a steady rhythm as she dug away at the wall.

When her finger punched through the wall, she stopped and peeked through the tiny hole she had created.

Below her was the steaming cauldron, and from this angle she could see the liquid inside rolling in a fast boil. It was definitely scalding hot.

She shifted her angle and looked farther into the room. Despite the bizarre scene of Dylan and his companion chained to the pillar, even more bizarre was the lack of the men in hoods who cast their shadows around the room.

One of the shadows glided across the floor until it was "standing" in front of Dylan.

The shadow on the floor shifted and then Dylan's head rocked to the side as if he had been slapped. He turned back to face forward, his face turning a bright red from the impact.

If these shadow creatures were able to

interact with Dylan then maybe the scalding water boiling in the cauldron would affect them as well.

It was the only plan she had, so she stuck with it.

She dug at the wall to hollow out most of it, leaving a small layer in place so as not to give away what she was doing before she was ready.

Chapter 2

Dylan opened his mouth wide and stretched his burning cheek.

"Owww…"

He looked straight ahead, but couldn't see anyone, or anything, in front of him. He glanced down to see the shadow of someone standing in front of him.

He looked back up to where he judged the face would be of whoever, or whatever, was standing there.

"Look, I don't know who you are, or what you want, but I am on a very important mission and you need to let me go."

His head jerked to the side from the

unexpected impact. He looked forward again into the seemingly empty room.

"Stop that!"

The man tied next to him leaned in close.

"You can stop pleading with them, they won't listen."

"What are they?"

"They are called Sciamachy. They are a race of shadows. It is futile to fight against them. Or resist."

"Are they indestructible?"

"No, but you can't see them, only the shadows they cast. They never fight in direct sunlight, but in the shade where they can hide and blend in with the natural shadows. That is why they were able to grab us so easily. We were in their domain."

Dylan flexed his aching jaw.

"But they are real. I'm pretty sure I hurt one of them when they grabbed us."

"You probably did, which is why they are punishing you before killing you."

"Punishing me?"

"I don't see them hitting me across the face."

"So I'm supposed to accept that I am their prisoner and I'm about to die?"

The man shrugged.

"That would be the easiest, yes."

Dylan looked back out into the empty room, the shadows dancing around the floor cast by the flickering light of the torches on the walls. He looked back at his companion.

"Then you don't know me at all. I don't

do things the easy way."

A scraping sound drew Dylan's attention to his right and he saw a wheeled cart carrying a large cone shaped brass instrument that looped around itself multiple times until it expanded into a large bell opening rolling toward him.

The cart stopped in front of him with the bell opening facing him.

Dylan looked at his companion.

"What is this?"

The man shook his head.

"I don't know. I've never seen it before."

Was Dylan staring into the business end of some kind of weapon?

Was this how he was going to die?

Just then, the wall on the far side of the

room crumbled inward accompanied by a rebel yell as someone burst through the wet dirt and jumped into the room.

Dylan instantly recognized the green tint of Larissa skin and smiled to himself. He wasn't going to be dying today.

Larissa grabbed the lip of the cauldron and overturned it, spilling the boiling contents onto the floor.

Shadows darted around in a panic as they ran in all directions trying to avoid the tiny tsunami of scalding liquid as it spread into the room.

Larissa jumped onto the cauldron and watched as the shadows funneled out of the room through the grate, leaving her alone in the room with Dylan and his friend.

Dylan's foot suddenly burned at the same moment his companion let out a yelp of surprise.

He pulled on the chains that bound him to the ceiling and lifted his feet off the floor as far as his bindings to the pillar would let him.

Looking down, he noted that steam rose up from the searing liquid as it traveled across the floor.

Within a few moments, the steam lessened as the liquid cooled from being spread thinly throughout the room.

When the liquid looked cool enough Larissa jumped off the overturned cauldron and ran over to Dylan.

She smiled at him with her jaggedly sharp

teeth.

"Happy to see me?" she asked.

He smiled back.

"What do you think?"

She reached up and yanked the chains out of the ceiling. Bits of dirt and rocked rained down on them.

She did the same for the other man before she twisted and broke open the wrist cuffs with her strong hands and freed them both from their shackles.

"We need to…" she started to say before she got a funny look on her face. Her eyes glazed over right before she pitched forward into Dylan's arms and went limp.

Dylan looked past her at the thick group of shadows that had come back into the

room.

He didn't see what suddenly jabbed him sharply in the arm, but he immediately felt the effects of the poison as it spread into the rest of his body.

The room blurred and he dropped Larissa as the floor rose up to smack him hard in the face.

Maybe today was the day he would die.

Chapter 3

The Spider Jockey yanked on the rope around Andre's wrists causing him to stumble forward. He caught his balance and didn't give the soldiers riding high on their spiders the satisfaction of him falling to his knees.

"Easy," he muttered under his breath as the soldier tugged on the ropes again to prod him to walk faster.

He had given up when they had surrounded him. He had let them tie him up and then watched in silence as they took his satchel and dumped the contents on the floor.

They seemed most interested in the medallion that Herobrine had given to Suzy, Josh, and him before they had entered the mountain on the other side.

He had told them that this was his symbol, and when they came across friends of his, they could use it to get help, food, and medical aide, or whatever they needed.

Herobrine had said that his influence spread far and wide, and anyone who knew him would benefit from having this medallion.

Rather than wear it around his neck like Suzy and Josh had done, Andre shoved it into his bag and promptly forgot about it.

As soon as the sparkly armored strangers found it in his bag, they looked up at him and sneered. These must not be friends of Herobrine because they tied him up and forced him to walk to who knows where instead of offering him a treat.

Several times he had tried to convince them to let him ride on one of their spiders, but they ignored him and only moved faster, forcing him to jog to keep from being pulled over by the rope around his wrists.

Andre shook his head.

Ever since coming to this Minecraft world, he had been forced to walk everywhere. Mountains, deserts, valleys, even underground.

It didn't seem to matter that he used to be able to fly, because Josh never figured it out and they had been forced to walk everywhere anyway.

His only consolation was that at least it was cool down here.

Suzy and Josh were probably still walking under a blistering hot desert sun.

Chapter 4

Suzy gripped the edge of the mine cart as it wheeled down the twisting underground tunnel. Ever since the cart had turned off the long and straight tunnel, they had entered a virtual roller coaster and careened through a winding track at incredible speeds.

Behind her, Josh sat on the floor and clung to a hand rail. He tried desperately to keep his ankle from banging against the side of the cart every time they took a tight turn. It didn't always work and he sucked in air quickly between his teeth each time the cart tossed him around.

With the distance they had been covering,

at least they weren't walking. They would never have been able to travel this far on foot, especially with Josh's twisted ankle.

At first, Suzy could tell that they were still heading in the direction they were walking on the surface, but after the first few turns, she had become completely turned around and had no idea which way they were traveling.

And they had been traveling for several hours and had to be hundreds of miles away from the desert by now.

They passed another corner that looked the same as every corner they had passed countless times before when a jarring thought occurred to her.

She lowered herself down next to Josh.

"Do you still have that red dye we picked up in the marketplace back when we first met Larissa?"

"Yea, why?"

"Give it to me."

Josh reached into his bag and produced a smaller bag closed tight with a drawstring.

"What do you want with it?"

"Just testing a theory."

She stood back up and watched the walls pass by in a blur.

When they reached a corner that looked like one they always made a left turn around, she threw the tiny bag out of the cart. It hit the corner and exploded in a crimson dust cloud, marking the corner with its bright red powder.

Suzy settled onto the edge of the cart and watched as they rocketed through more tunnels and turned even more corners, going in random directions each time.

As they continued through more random tunnels and took random corners she counted out the seconds.

When she had counted out enough seconds to equal ten minutes, she saw a bright red flash coming up fast.

The cart turned to the left around the same corner she had hit with the bag of red dye ten minutes before.

They kept careening around corners and rocketing down tunnels while she counted again.

Once she had counted out ten minutes

again, she saw the flash of red coming up fast.

And then they turned left around the same corner and kept going.

She wished she had been wrong, but there was no denying what was happening.

They were going in circles.

She slid down the side and sat in the cart trying to think.

But why were they being taken in circles for so long?

Was someone trying to figure out what to do with them, and by keeping the two of them occupied, it would give their unseen benefactors some time to decide?

Well, it had worked. It had taken her too long to determine they weren't really going anywhere.

She stood up in the cart again and screamed at the top of her lungs.

"If you can hear me, we know you haven't taken us anywhere, and we would like to get off this ride now."

Josh sat up.

"Who are you talking to?"

She looked down at him.

"We've been going in circles."

He looked around him at the tunnel walls in alarm.

"What?"

She pointed ahead of them at the flash of red that was coming up right on schedule.

"We've been passing that same spot every ten minutes. We really haven't gone anywhere. How's your ankle?"

He touched it softly and winced.

"I guess I can walk on it if I have to."

She remained standing and started to lean into the turn as they reached the corner she had marked. She almost fell out of the mine cart when it turned unexpectedly to the right and threw her off balance.

After taking this new turn, the cart shot down a straight tunnel without taking any turns at all.

For the first time since they had climbed into the cart, they were finally going somewhere.

Suzy sat next to Josh as the cart wheeled down the track at high speed. She tenderly touched Josh's ankle.

"How's it feeling?"

Josh rubbed it, wincing a little bit.

"It's getting better."

They had only been traveling for ten minutes when the cart slowed down and they looked at each other. Suzy stood up enough to peek over the rim of the open cart.

The track ended a few hundred feet ahead of them, and there were dozens of soldiers dressed in black armor that shimmered in the light. The soldiers were waiting for them with swords and spears drawn and ready.

Suzy dropped back down next to Josh.

"Out of the frying pan and into the fire," she said.

Josh gave her a quizzical look.

She smiled sadly at him.

"Are you ready to deal with more armed soldiers?"

"Not with this ankle."

She nodded as the cart came to a full stop.

Together, they stood up, raising their hands in the air in surrender.

The soldiers all looked at Josh in shock and immediately dropped to one knee at the same time, bowing their heads to look at the floor.

The lead soldier closest to the cart raised his head slightly, looking at the base of the cart instead of at Suzy and Josh.

"Our deepest apologies, Sir. We did not know it was you."

Chapter 5

The first sensation Larissa experienced was how thick and bloated her tongue felt inside her mouth. A half-second later, she could see the wash of red as her eyes noted the awareness of light behind her closed eyelids.

She opened her mouth and raked her dry tongue across cracked lips.

She felt a guiding hand on the back of her head lift her up slowly. The wet rim of a cup brushed against her lips and she opened her mouth instinctively to allow the cool liquid to quench her thirst before she dared to open her eyes.

When she had her fill, she pulled away from the cup and was lowered slowly back to the soft pillow.

She opened her eyes and blinked at the sudden brightness. She looked at the ceiling above her, and then risked the dizziness to look around her.

She could feel the leather straps that held her fast to the bed she was lying in. She could easily break through the straps with her zombie strength, but decided to wait and see what she had gotten herself into before making her escape.

She glanced around the room. Except for the closed door and window, there were only two other pieces of furniture in the room beside her bed. A chair and a strange brass horn on a wheeled cart that coiled around itself dozens of times.

Whoever had just given her a drink of water must have rushed out of the room. The chair next to her bed was empty.

She turned her head the other direction and froze. The bright light streaming in from the window showed two dark silhouettes on the wall. She could clearly see the lump of shadow that was her lying in bed. But she could also see the shadow of someone sitting in the chair next to the bed.

When she looked back at the chair, it was still empty. This time, she looked down to the floor and saw additional shadows beyond the legs of the chair. There was a faint shadow made by the feet and legs of someone sitting in the chair.

The large brass horn on the pushcart rolled over next to the bed of its own accord. More likely, whoever was in the chair had pulled it close to the bed.

The bell of the horn pointed directly at Larissa. She could feel the vibrations coming from the horn before any sound reached her ears.

She tensed, squeezing her eyes shut, not sure what was about to happen.

What did happen made her eyes pop open in surprise.

The faint whisper of an airy voice rose in pitch slowly as it echoed from deep within the bell of the horn, the first syllable of the first word drawn out like a ghost was speaking to her.

"Hhhhhow are you feeling?"

Larissa stared at the wider end of the horn, her eyebrows knitted in confusion.

The voice echoed again from inside the horn, the first syllable of the first word was again stretched out eerily.

"Yyyyyou can hear me? Yes?"

Larissa nodded and glanced back and forth between the empty chair and the horn.

"It's okay," the voice whispered. "We are used to people talking to the horn. I will not be insulted."

Larissa glanced back at the chair, but turned to the horn before speaking.

"What… who are you?"

"We are known by many names. Some

call us angels while others call us demons. The most descriptive name was given to us a long time ago. We are the Sciamachy, it means to fight a shadow or an imaginary enemy. You may call us by that name."

Larissa shook her head. The pain behind her eyes screamed at the sudden motion and she stopped moving.

"What is your name?"

There was a slight pause before the faint sound echoed up from the horn.

"My name is Essence."

"Why can't I see you?"

"Our scientists gave up a long time ago on trying to determine why we are invisible, yet still cast shadows. It is what it is and we have come to accept that."

Larissa stared at the empty chair then returned her attention back to the bell of the horn. It was easier to talk to something she could see.

"How come I've never heard about you?"

"We stay in the shadows of legends and myths. It is better for us to remain hidden."

"Then why did you capture my friend?"

"You mean the loudmouthed man?"

Larissa smiled. It didn't take Dylan long to build a reputation when it didn't have the chance to precede him.

"Yeah, that sounds like Dylan."

"He invaded our world. We were only defending ourselves."

"Invaded your world?"

When the silence stretched on and it was

evident that the horn would remain silent, Larissa pushed further.

"How did he invade, I thought he was escaping from the prison cells?"

There was no response from the horn.

"Essence? Are you still there?"

The sound built up from a faint whisper in a crescendo until Larissa could make out what was being said on the other side of the horn. It sounded like Essence was talking to someone else, but she only heard Essence's side of the conversation.

"I don't want to hurt her... yes, Sir... of course... I understand."

Larissa turned her head away from the horn and could see two shadows, one sitting in the chair and the other standing next to the bed. She could still hear Essence through the horn.

"It will be done."

The standing shadow moved closer to the door. Larissa looked over in time to see the door open and close all by itself.

Larissa looked at the empty chair.

"Essence," Larissa said quietly.

There was no response from the horn so Larissa spoke louder this time.

"Essence!"

"I'm sorry."

Essence's voice had come so faintly from the horn, Larissa wasn't sure she had heard anything.

And just then, the door opened and closed again.

"Essence!" Larissa screamed.

"Essence!" she screamed even louder.

Larissa turned to look at the far wall and saw only her shadow lying on the bed.

She was alone.

It was time to leave.

She strained at the straps, but they held her tightly to the bed.

She flexed her arms and took a deep breath, expanding her body to push against the straps.

They were stronger than she was expecting. She had to arch her back, pushing harder as the edges of the straps dug into her arms and legs.

She gritted her teeth against the pain and forced herself to push harder.

The slight tearing sound rewarded her efforts, so she pushed even more, ignoring the pain.

A ripping sound, accompanied by the sudden loosening of the straps, meant she was finally free of her restraints.

She sat up and immediately regretted it.

The wave of dizziness sent the room into a flat tailspin.

She gripped the edge of the bad and closed her eyes to re-center herself.

When the room stopped spinning, she opened her eyes slowly and swung her feet over the edge.

She took two quick breaths, stood unsteadily on her feet, and wobbled as she stood next to the bed.

She quickly scanned the room, relieved to see that her shadow was the only one on the wall.

She still had to find Dylan and the Crystal Cube before she could get out of... where was she?

She stumbled to the window, the only gateway to the outside, and peered through it.

She didn't know what to expect when she looked through the window. But what she saw was not even close to anything she ever would have expected.

Chapter 6

Andre wasn't really paying attention to where he was going as he walked and ended up bumping into the lead Spider Jockey who had stopped in front of him. The spider reacted and shuffled nervously back and forth. The armored rider pulled hard on the reins to calm it down.

The armored soldier on the spider behind him called out.

"What is it Caiden?"

Caiden twisted in his saddle and looked back at the soldier behind Andre. The look on his face was one of terror and he pointed ahead of him.

The soldier directly behind Andre stood up in his saddle and looked past Caiden. When he frowned, Andre leaned to the side to look around the giant spider and see what he was looking at.

The tunnel ahead was pitch black.

Caiden glanced into the blackened abyss and back at the other soldier.

"What happened to the lights, Kamron?"

Kamron, the soldier on the spider behind Andre, shrugged his shoulders.

One of the other two of the Spider Jockeys behind Kamron called down the tunnel.

"Why did we stop?"

Kamron turned around.

"The tunnel lights are out ahead."

"Why didn't maintenance fix them?" a Spider Jockey asked.

Kamron shook his head and turned back around, muttering under his breath.

Andre couldn't make out exactly what he said, but he obviously wasn't pleased with the stupid question from the soldier behind him.

Andre saw his chance and looked directly at Kamron.

"You guys afraid of the dark?" he said with a sneer.

Kamron gave him a steely gaze.

"You would be too if you knew what was hiding in there. It is not the dark we are worried about."

Kamron shifted his gaze to Caiden.

Caiden nodded and pulled on the reins of his spider.

"We're turning around. We'll take another path."

The soldiers spun their spiders around and Andre had to hustle to keep from being pulled off his feet as he ran around to get behind Caiden's spider.

Andre jogged next to Caiden who rode up on the side of the wall to get past the other soldiers and their spiders. Andre kept his hands raised above his head as he squeezed past the other three spiders and tried not to let them see him flinch as he bumped into jittery spider legs.

As soon as Caiden was past them, he came back down to the floor and Andre could lower his arms.

Andre glanced back at the other three soldiers; that all held an assorted variety of weapons at the ready.

What were these soldiers afraid of?

He glanced past them to the darkened tunnel that receded as they moved quickly down the tunnel away from it.

As he looked behind him, another panel of lights began to flicker, and went out.

Andre frowned, the lines on his forehead creasing deeper as he kept watching the tunnel behind them while letting the ropes pull him.

The next set of torches along the wall flickered and went out as well.

Whatever had knocked the lights out was

following them, and taking out the next set of torches as they got closer.

Andre focused on Kamron riding behind him and nodded behind them with his head.

"Hey! The torches are going out."

Kamron looked at him.

"What?"

"The torches in the tunnel behind us, they are going out."

Kamron twisted in his saddle and watched as the next set of torches flickered and died.

Kamron spun back around and his face was ashen.

"Sciamachy!" he yelled.

Andre was about to ask what a "say-um-uh-key" was when he was immediately jerked forward. He struggled to stay on his feet as he ran behind Caiden's spider at a fast clip.

"Guys?" Andre said between ragged breaths.

"Guys!" he said again.

Caiden spun around and yanked on the rope, pulling Andre closer to his running spider, until Andre was between the rear legs that moved in a blur on either side of him.

Caiden reached his hand out, offering it to Andre. Andre took it and Caiden pulled him onto the back of his spider.

Caiden gave him a stern look.

"Sit down, shut up, and hang on."

Andre glanced back to see the torches going out at a rate faster than they were moving.

The rear Spider Jockey was engulfed by

darkness right before he let out a blood curdling scream and then fell silent.

This made the remaining three Spider Jockeys kick their spiders in their sides with the heels of their boots, urging them to run faster.

Andre clung to Caiden's back like a motorcycle passenger and glanced back just as the torches went out, plunging the rear Spider Jockey into darkness.

Andre focused on the blackness and waited for the scream.

The rear rider shot out into the light, moving faster. Andre was about to smile when he thought he saw a shadow on the wall dart forward and pull the rider off his spider.

The torches went out before the rider hit the ground and Andre couldn't see what happened to him, but his imagination presented him with all sorts of terrible fates.

The only sounds that echoed through the tunnels were the pitter-patter of spider legs running briskly across the ground.

There was no hint of who was following them, or who was putting out the torches, or who was attacking the soldiers.

It was if they were being chased by the shadows themselves.

But that was ridiculous. Even in this artificial world created by a game programmer. Notch had designed this world to mimic the real world, and as far as Andre knew, monsters in the dark were only stories told by R.L. Stine to scare little kids.

They didn't chase you down a dark tunnel.

Even if you were racing down that same tunnel on the back of a giant spider.

The torches going out behind them began to catch up with Kamron. He didn't look back; the look on Andre's face told him everything he needed to know.

"Get to the surface," Kamron yelled as the darkness caught up with him and he was flung off the back of his spider by some unseen force.

Andre turned back and yelled into Caiden's ear.

"They're all gone."

Caiden didn't turn around to verify Andre's claim. It was like he already knew it would happen and was willing to believe his prisoner.

Caiden leaned forward in his saddle and kicked the sides of his spider.

The spider responded by speeding up, taking corners at high speed as it darted back and forth through the intersecting tunnels.

Andre risked a peek behind them and noticed that the tunnel was still lit behind them. A moment later, the torch went out, but they were leaving whatever had attacked the rest of the soldiers farther behind with each passing second.

They were getting away.

Suddenly, Caiden slowed down and came to a full stop.

Andre looked at Caiden with alarm.

"Why did you stop? We were getting away!"

Caiden hopped off the spider and yanked Andre off with a tug of the ropes that still bound him at the wrists.

Andre tumbled off the spider and landed hard on his back, the wind knocked out of him.

Caiden reached down and untied the ropes, releasing Andre. Andre looked at his free hands and then at Caiden.

"You're letting me go?"

Caiden smiled at him and reached up to unlatch a hatch in the ceiling of the tunnel.

The hatch dropped open and a ladder extended down to the floor with a rattling clanking sound.

Caiden mounted the ladder and started climbing. As soon as he was through the hatch, Andre approached the ladder, but before he could grab it, it receded back up into the ceiling.

"Hey!" he yelled up into the open hatch.

Caiden popped his head down.

"What?"

"Send the ladder back down."

"Sorry. No can do."

Caiden reached down and grabbed the handle on the inside of the hatch and started pulling it closed.

Andre grabbed the edge of the hatch and held it in place.

"Let me up."

Caiden looked down the tunnel and then

disappeared up through the hatch. His foot suddenly appeared and kicked at Andre's fingers, scraping them painfully off the edge of the hatch.

With Andre no longer holding the hatch, it continued upward on its springs and clicked shut.

Andre reached up, trying to pry open the hatch, but it was locked from the inside.

His peripheral vision registered something to his left and he looked in time to see the farthest torch flicker and go out.

He took a couple steps backward as the next closer torch went out.

Chapter 7

Josh and Suzy looked at each other. A devious smile spread across her lips as she nodded at the bowing soldiers.

Josh looked back at the leader.

"Now that you know who I am, I expect to be treated with a little more respect."

The leader stood up and snapped to attention, the rest of the soldiers following his motion.

"Of course, Sir. We live only to serve Herobrine."

The leader turned to a soldier to his right.

"Contact Caiden immediately, tell him who he has tied up, and order him to release

Herobrine before we suffer the consequences."

Josh's and Suzy's heads snapped toward each other. Her smile faded and turned to one of concern. Had they found Herobrine and saved him from the spider?

Josh looked back at the leader of the soldiers.

"I am hungry and tired."

The leader bowed his head again.

"Of course. We will fulfill your desires."

Two soldiers helped Josh out of the cart and supported him as he hobbled on his ankle.

The leader stood in front of Josh at attention.

"My name is Commander Janssen of the

Shadow Warriors. Our doctors will look at your injury and provide a healing solution. You will be in the best care."

Josh smiled at him.

"Thank you."

Janssen smiled back.

"Of course, Sir. You must be ready."

Suzy stepped closer.

"Ready for what?"

Janssen looked at her.

"Your companion and his other self must be united to fulfill the prophecy."

Josh frowned.

"Other self? Prophecy?"

Janssen turned and pointed toward the door that led away from the mine cart platform.

"All in due time. First you must be healed, rested, and fed."

Another Shadow Warrior rushed up to Janssen and whispered into his ear. Janssen nodded to him.

"Get him back."

The other warrior rushed off, calling to other warriors to follow him.

Suzy watched the Shadow Warriors run away before looking at Janssen.

"What's going on?"

Instead of answering Suzy directly, Janssen looked at Josh as he replied.

"It appears your other self has been captured by the Sciamachy. Don't worry. My men will get him back."

Janssen's eyes glazed over as he seemed to

look through Josh.

"Or die trying."

Chapter 8

Andre struggled against invisible forces that had tied him up, or at least it felt like he was tied up. He couldn't see what bound his hands together, but he felt the tug as someone, or something, pulled him forward through the darkness.

For everything he had dealt with since coming into this world, Andre had never been as afraid for his life as he was now.

But why was he afraid? They couldn't kill him. All that would happen if they tried was that he would wake up in the chair back in his dad's lab.

He would be fine.

But it would mean that he had failed.

Failed to prevent a computer program from destroying the world and enslaving humanity.

That was what frightened him the most.

He wasn't afraid of death.

He was afraid of failure.

So how could he keep from becoming a failure?

By not giving up, that's how.

He flexed his hands against the invisible rope. Maybe he could still turn this around? Maybe he could break free and make a run for it?

He glanced behind him before looking forward. The tunnels were dark in every direction. It was no use. Even if he managed to escape his unseen restraints, and avoid the hidden forces who held him captive, it was too dark to be running around in the tunnels.

He needed some form of light source if he planned to make a run for it.

Ahead of them was inky blackness. He couldn't run forward, so he would have to make his way back the way they had come if he broke away.

He glanced behind him again and did a double-take when he spotted a pinpoint of light bobbing up and down rushing toward them.

The invisible people must have seen it too because he was nearly yanked off his feet when they jerked roughly on his restraints and pulled him faster through the tunnel.

He struggled against them, digging his heels into the floor. Whoever the invisible people were running from was someone he wanted to let catch up, and he would do whatever it took to help his potential saviors.

His foot caught on a seam in the floor tiles and he pitched forward face first.

Invisible hands grabbed him and kept him from smashing his face on the dusty ground.

He was lifted into the air and bent in half, like someone had just tossed him over their shoulder like a sack of potatoes.

Andre's teeth rattled as he was jostled around as whoever was carrying him ran at a fast pace.

Andre lifted his head to look behind and could see the pinpoint light was bigger and had resolved itself into a flickering torch held in a hand he could actually see.

Whoever was coming wasn't invisible.

Unfortunately, as the light got closer, he could see that the arm that held the torch high in the air was encased by the sparkling black armor of his first captors.

Andre was the rope in a tug-of-war battle between two unknown enemies, both intent on being the victor.

The torch got ever closer and Andre could make out the faint blur of spider legs illuminated by the flickering flame. Behind the first torch were dozens of new pinpoints of light.

Despite not being able to see their enemy, the armored soldiers must have decided to send everyone in the hopes of outnumbering their foe.

It was a scare tactic that worked very well on Andre. He hoped it worked on whoever was carrying him over their shoulder through the underground tunnels.

Andre watched as the lead soldier on the spider took out a slingshot and shot a small white ball. When it hit the ceiling above Andre, white powder exploded to completely fill the tunnel in a choking cloud.

Andre slammed his eyes shut and coughed as he breathed in the white powder that engulfed him.

He felt his captor slip on the slick powder that filtered quickly to the floor.

He looked down and couldn't see who

carried him, as such, but he could see the outline of a man dusted fully in white powder along with two more ghostlike figures running behind him.

Andre craned his neck around. But there were only the three white ghosts with him.

He was sure there had been more, with how easily they had dispatched the soldiers with him earlier.

But then again, being invisible probably increased their combat efficiency by a factor of ten to one.

Looking behind him, he could see the armored soldiers getting closer and drawing their swords.

With the powder explosion in the tunnel, the invisible enemy wasn't invisible anymore.

The Spider Jockeys were gaining on them. They didn't stand a chance against the twenty armed soldiers coming in fast on the backs of spiders.

His captors must have suspected as much.

Andre's stomach lurched as he was flung to the ground. He stuck his hands out to break his fall, but it didn't work out as well as he wanted.

He hit the ground and smacked the side of his head, sending shooting pain down his spine and producing stars that bloomed in his vision. It was not at all funny like the stars that circled a character's head in the cartoons.

Andre slid on the floor and came to rest against the wall as the Spider Jockeys thundered past him in pursuit of the running ghosts.

A spider stopped in front of Andre. Feet jumped down into his view and walked over to where he was lying on the floor.

Andre looked up at the smiling face of Caiden, the warrior who had abandoned him at the hatch.

Caiden reached down to lift Andre to his feet.

"Sorry about leaving you back there. I needed a chance to rally the troops to combat the Sciamachy, and I couldn't do that with you fighting me every step of the way."

Andre pulled his hands out of Caiden's grip.

"So you just thought you'd leave me back there?"

Caiden shrugged.

"It worked didn't it? I got you back."

Andre looked down the tunnel at the Spider Jockeys that chased down the white figures.

"I don't know if that's better or worse."

Caiden wrapped a new rope around Andre's hands and made sure it was secure before hopping up onto his spider.

"It's better, trust me."

"Says the guy who just tied me back up."

"Can't have you trying to run off. You have a destiny to fulfill, and it is my responsibility to make sure you do it."

"What destiny? What are you talking

about?"

Caiden smiled as he turned his spider around and tugged on the ropes.

"Come along Herobrine, we have your other half. When you are joined, you will be useful to us once again."

Andre was too stunned to respond as he let Caiden lead him by the ropes down the tunnel.

Had Caiden just called him Herobrine?

None of his captors had taken the time to ask him who he was. Maybe that was because they thought they already knew.

But why did they think he was Herobrine?

It didn't make sense.

Both groups had tied him up and treated him like a prisoner.

What had Herobrine done to these people?

Whatever it was, it seemed that Andre was going to be the one punished for his crimes.

It seemed an ironic fate.

He had come into this world to stop Herobrine, and now he was being led to meet some horrible fate as if he were Herobrine himself.

Chapter 9

Josh and Suzy were led to a small room and ushered inside. When the door closed, Josh heard the locks engage.

Suzy rushed to the door and pushed and pulled. She gave up and leaned her back against the door.

"It's no use. It's locked."

Josh lowered himself to the floor and shook his head at her.

"Duh, Sherlock. I heard the locks too."

He scratched at the edge of the cast the Shadow Warrior's doctor had placed around his ankle. Suzy came over and bent down over the cast.

"How does it feel?"

"It actually tickles more than it hurts. Whatever that sticky green slime was they smeared on it before sealing it in this cast seems to be working."

She looked around the small room. There was only a single window. She stood up.

"Just rest."

She walked over to the window and looked out. Outside was a large sand covered arena with several soldiers and gladiators all sparring with each other while others looked on and gave pointers on how to vanquish their foe better.

She scanned the entire arena, trying to find a familiar face amongst the strangers that filled the battle space when her mouth fell open in shock.

Looking at her from a similar window across the wide open arena was Larissa.

Chapter 10

Larissa wiped at the window with her sleeve, not sure if what she was seeing was real or not.

The window looked out onto a large open area where gladiators and warriors were sparring against each other.

And on the far side of the dusty arena she could see Suzy in the window of a room similar to hers.

Larissa smiled and waved.

Suzy waved back, the look on her face showing she was just as stunned as Larissa was to see each other in the same place.

They had taken off in opposite directions,

and now they were back together again.

Larissa mouthed, "Where's Herobrine?"

Suzy squinted at her and mimicked that she didn't understand what she was asking before suddenly looking back into her room and disappearing from the window.

As soon as Suzy disappeared, Larissa heard the door to her prison unlock.

She spun around as two shadows silently glided along the wall. She felt rough hands grab her, but she didn't struggle and let them take her wherever they were planning to take her.

She was whisked down the hallway and into another room. She was roughly tossed into a chair and held down by unseen hands.

Along the back wall were various weapons

of increasing lethality. She saw several pieces of sparking black armor float toward her.

She was lifted back to a standing position and the armor layered around her body. When the armor was secured, she was let go and a faint voice echoed out to her from the horn sitting on a table next to the chair.

"Select a weapon."

She looked around the empty room before focusing on the wider end of the horn.

"A weapon? Why?"

"You have been chosen to fight."

She looked around the room. It was unnerving to talk to someone you couldn't see.

"Fight?"

"Select a weapon," the voice repeated.

She looked at the wall loaded with implements of terror and death. She turned back to the horn and placed her hands defiantly on her hips.

"No."

"Suit yourself, but you will be battling against two able warriors…" there was a pause before the voice continued.

"You will be battling three formidable foes on your own. We tried to select a warrior to stand by your side, but we were not successful. You will stand alone and the armor will only protect you for so long. You should arm yourself and prepare for battle."

A piece of red chalk floated off the table and drew a line across the floor to another door on the other side of the room.

The voice continued from deep within the horn.

"When that door opens, the competition will begin."

"Why are you doing this?"

"You are the perfect warrior to fight for us. We have seen your kind before. They are difficult to kill. We feel confident that, despite the three to one odds against you, you will be victorious."

"What do I get if I win?"

"You are fighting for your life and for your freedom, so I suggest you work quickly to reduce the enemy before you tire out."

A tone echoed loudly through the walls.

"There is only one minute before the

battle begins."

A helmet floated toward her. She held her neck steady as it was lowered over her head and locked into place.

Along one side stood a full-length mirror and she turned one way and then another, taking in her reflection.

The armor covered her entire body, layered like the scales of a dragon, leaving no part of her green flesh exposed. The helmet, while not overly large, fit her head perfectly as if it was crafted specifically for her.

She looked again at the wall of weapons and took down a jagged edged sword that curved like a shiny crescent moon.

She swung it around several times, marveling at the balance and how light it was.

"Excellent choice," the voice intoned through the horn. With a click, the section of wall with the weapons on it receded inward, the wall closing around it and snapping shut like a closet.

Another loud tone reverberated through the walls and the door she had been dragged through opened and closed quickly. She knew it was her invisible captors leaving her alone, so she didn't bother to ask the horn any more questions.

A loud click behind her drew her attention to the other door as it swung slowly open, groaning on rusty hinges.

When the door was open, she peered out through it. Beyond the door was the arena she had seen earlier. Only this time, the groups of gladiators and soldiers were gone, leaving an empty arena.

On the other side of the arena, she saw another door open slowly and three soldiers stepped out into the arena. They were dressed in the same scaled armor she was in, complete with enclosing helmets. As they walked out, they looked in her direction.

It hardly seemed fair that she was pitted against three others, but then again, with the increased strength given to her by the zombie blood coursing through her veins, maybe it wasn't a fair fight for the other three.

She stepped into the arena and her door slammed shut behind her. She saw the door on the other side slam shut behind the third warrior just as he stepped through.

They were both in the same situation, but only one side would be victorious.

Larissa hunched down and held her crescent sword at the ready.

They could very well have sent in three hundred warriors to fight with her in this arena.

She already knew one fact that could never be changed.

She wasn't going to be the one to lose today.

Chapter 11

Josh limped out through the door, dressed fully in the same shining black armor as the Shadow Warriors who had captured him, Andre, and Suzy. As soon as he was clear the door slammed shut behind him.

The reunion with Andre in the room had been short lived when they found out that they were going to be battling a Sciamachy warrior to the death.

Their only consolation was that they were assured that the Sciamachy's warrior would remain visible the entire time. It was part of the rules of the shaky alliance between the Sciamachy and the Shadow Warriors.

Their battle for territory was handled in the arena by their chosen warriors. The losers would lose a valiant warrior and the border would shift in favor of the winner.

For the past several arena battles, the Sciamachy had been gaining more land from the Shadow Warriors.

For this reason, they decided to send in three warriors to battle the Sciamachy's best warrior.

Unfortunately, the three they had picked to be their warriors in this battle were Josh, Andre, and Suzy.

On the other side of the arena from them was only one Sciamachy warrior.

Maybe they stood a chance if they worked together. He set all his weight on his bad ankle and was amazed that it felt fully healed.

The burning sensation had faded and he was able to apply his full weight on it with the pain staying suppressed as a dull ache. He limped when he walked on it, but the sharp, stabbing pain was gone.

He could probably run if he had to. The Shadow Warrior's doctors were amazing.

Now, if they only put this much thought into their armor and weapons, the three of them just might stand a chance against the challenger across the arena who swayed back and forth, apparently preparing to charge forward and attack.

Suzy glanced sideways at him.

"Are you okay?"

Josh nodded.

"I'll feel better when this is all over."

Andre sidled up next to him.

"Do you think they want us to kill him?"

As if in answer to his question a booming voice echoed across the arena.

"Today's battle to the death is to determine the status of the northern border by five degrees."

Josh answered him.

"What do you think?"

Andre tossed down his sword.

"Then I refuse to fight."

Suzy glanced at him.

"What are you doing?"

Andre shook his head.

"I'm not doing it. I'm not playing their game."

Josh bent down and picked up the sword from the sand-covered floor. He held it out to Andre.

"That only works if you can get him to agree not to kill you."

Andre refused to take it from Josh.

"I don't care. Let him kill me if he wants. I'll just wake up back at Dad's office, safe and sound."

Suzy got in his face, her helmet touching his.

"We need you here with us."

"Why? Why do you need me?"

"To stop Mallory. We can't do it without you."

"Why not? You seem to be doing just fine without me all those other times."

Josh moved in closer.

"It will take all three of us to stop Mallory now that Herobrine is dead."

Andre looked at him.

"Is he? The soldiers told me that they had him and he was supposed to be in here to help us fight whatever that thing is." Andre punctuated his sentence by pointing to the warrior across the arena.

Suzy grabbed him and spun him to face her.

"We told you. I think they were making all that up. They told us they had Herobrine too, but we haven't seen him anywhere."

Andre glared at her, even though neither Suzy nor Josh could tell by anything other than his body language since the helmet hid his face.

"Maybe this is what Herobrine had in store for us in the first place. It's why he led us here and then disappeared in the tunnel before we got to this desolate place."

Suzy shook her head.

"Herobrine wouldn't do this to us. Besides, he was taken by the cave spider. We all saw it happen. You saw it happen."

"I don't know what I saw anymore. This world is not the real world. They can make us see anything we want."

"None of these people have control over the world. They live in it by the same rules we do."

"That's just it. I'm sick of living by the same rules. I want to make some of my own, starting with this stupid contest."

Andre spun around and walked back to the door. He tried to pry it open with his fingers, but it had sealed itself and was flush with the wall after closing.

He banged on it several times.

"Hey! Open up!" he yelled.

Josh took his eyes off of the warrior across the arena for only a second to glance at Andre pounding on the locked door.

When he looked back, the enemy was rushing toward them at high speed.

"Here he comes!" Josh yelled.

Chapter 12

Larissa had watched as one of the warriors dropped his sword and tried to be let out of the arena. The second warrior, distracted with dealing with the first one, left only one of them watching her.

Her muscles burned from the tension as she held her stance, ready to pounce at the most opportune time.

And when the third warrior glanced back to see what his companion was doing, that was her chance.

She sprang forward and rushed silently toward them, raising her curved sword above her head. She aimed for the third warrior, since he was the one who had remained the most vigilant when the first warrior had changed his mind and tried to get back through the door.

Suddenly, Larissa sprawled on the ground and slid to a stop on her side.

She looked back to see what she had tripped over and saw nothing.

She stood back up and suddenly felt pressure on her chest and the back of her leg at the same time as she flopped backward..

She rolled over quickly and got up quickly to her knees.

For the first time, she noticed the crowds gathered in rows of seats on the one side of the arena.

She glanced over at the other side to see

the entire seating area empty, yet darkened with shifting shadows.

It was filled with the invisible people who were using her to fight their war with the enemy.

She swung around and faced the three warriors on the opposing team.

All three of them were now trying to pry open the door.

She got to her feet and slowly walked toward them. As she got closer, one of them spotted her approaching and tapped the others on the back.

One by one the spun around slowly and faced her.

The bravest of them charged at her.

Fool!

Larissa noticed the shadow race across the ground right before the enemy combatant tripped over nothing and fell to the ground.

One of the invisible people was trying to prevent this fight.

But why?

A booming voice echoed in the arena.

"The combat shall continue without interference. Will the Sciamachy called Essence please leave the arena."

Larissa straightened up.

It was Essence who had tripped her and knocked her down. She was trying to prevent this fight.

Larissa scanned the ground until she saw the shadow, then looked up to where she thought Essence's eyes might be.

"I can't hear you without the horn, Essence," she said. And then a thought occurred to her.

"Draw on the ground."

Essence understood her and she watched as letters formed magically in the sand. The letters formed words:

THESE ARE YOUR FRIENDS

She looked up from the words at the three enemy soldiers.

Friends?

She saw them with new eyes. There were three of them, and she had recently seen Suzy in the window. Of course, a window to a room just like hers.

Could these three actually be Josh, Andre, and Suzy?

She dropped her crescent sword and struggled to remove her helmet. As she worked it off, the crowd began to boo and hiss loudly.

Once she had the helmet off, she faced the three with her green zombie face.

While she couldn't see their faces through the helmets, their body language said it all.

They all rushed at her as one to the growing cheers of the crowd. They were finally going to see some bloodshed.

When the three of them grabbed her in a big hug, and she hugged them back, the crowd fell silent.

One by one they ripped off their helmets and smiled at each other.

Larissa looked at all of them.

"What are you guys doing here?"

Suzy was the first to respond.

"We were taken by the Shadow Warriors under the desert and they brought us all the way back here. What are you doing here?"

"I was following Dylan when the invisible people grabbed us."

Larissa looked at the twins.

"Where's Herobrine?"

Andre looked down at the ground and Josh's face fell. Josh cleared his throat to say something when Andre pointed at the floor.

"Look!"

A hatch had opened up, dropping away into the darkness, sand spilling in after it around the edges.

Written next to the opening was one word

and an arrow pointing to the hatch.

QUICKLY

It was then that Larissa noticed that the crowd had become angered and was yelling for all of them to be put to death.

In answer to the crowds growing unrest, soldiers started to spill out from the iron gates along the walls.

Larissa pointed to the soldiers coming at the small group of friends.

I guess we better do as Essence says."

"Who's Essence," Andre asked.

Larissa shoved him ahead of her into the open hatch.

"No time. Go!"

Chapter 13

Josh was the last one through the opening in the floor. As he jumped into the hole, he saw the closest soldier trip and fall, the rest landing on top of him.

Just then, something brushed past him, pulled him through the opening, and pushed the hatch closed. It locked with a solid click and a torch lifted off the wall to float in the air.

The torch rushed to the front of the line and continued down the dark tunnel.

Larissa pointed toward the receding torch. "Follow her."

Josh stood stock still, staring at the

floating torch.

"What is that?"

Larissa shoved him forward.

"Just follow the torch."

A loud banging sound echoed from the sealed hatch. Larissa looked at it briefly before pointing down the tunnel.

"Follow it now!"

Andre and Suzy rushed after the torch while Josh hobbled on his cast. The pain had subsided and he no longer felt his injured ankle. He hobbled now because of the bulkiness of the cast on his foot.

The torch took them through several twists and turns, making intersection choices seemingly at random.

Josh was having a hard time keeping up

due to the cast.

Suddenly, the torch stopped in the middle of the tunnel and worked its way back to where Josh stood and then past him.

The torch moved back and forth closely against the wall.

Larissa stood next to Josh.

"What is it, Essence?"

The torch waved back and forth quickly before moving alongside the wall at a steady pace.

"Essence?" Larissa asked.

The torch stopped when the flame flickered slightly. It waved back and forth in front of a small seam in the wall panels. As it did, the flame flickered as if being blown by a brisk wind.

The torch dropped to the floor and the panel started separating from the rest of the wall slowly.

It pulled out half an inch before snapping back into place.

A half-second later, the panel pulled out again along one edge.

"Help her," Larissa hollered as she jumped forward and stuck her fingers in the opening made by the panel.

Suzy and Andre moved forward, but there wasn't enough room for both of them and Andre stepped back to watch Larissa and Suzy wrench the panel off the wall.

Once removed, they could see the smaller tunnel that led away from the tunnel they were in.

The torch lifted off the floor and scooted into the smaller tunnel.

This time Josh moved quickly, not wanting to be the last one in the group again.

As he followed the torch, he noted that it scooted on the ground and then stopped before scooting again, like someone was holding it in one hand and crawling through the tunnel. This new tunnel was half as tall as the first tunnel so he copied what the invisible girl was doing and dropped to his hands and knees.

He couldn't see whoever was holding the torch, only the shadow they cast from the flickering light of the fire.

It was spooky.

As well as being invisible, the unknown

person made absolutely no sound whatsoever. All he could hear from whoever they were following was the scraping of the torch on the ground as she crawled through the low tunnel ahead of the group.

Up ahead, the tunnel turned at a right angle. Josh, Andre, Suzy, and Larissa all following the torch as it scraped across the ground around several more turns until it stopped at another grate.

The grate swung open and the torch floated out of the tunnel.

Josh followed the torch quickly into the large room, glad to be out of the cramped space. Andre, Suzy, and Larissa all hopped down into the room, their shadows dancing on the wall by the flicker of torchlight.

Josh arched his back and stretched, pausing in surprise as the shadows on the wall showed more people in this room than he could see directly.

Chapter 14

Dylan ran a rough tongue around his dry mouth. He smacked his lips loudly, trying to prompt his saliva glands to remedy his parched state.

Well, he thought, at least he wasn't dead.

When his mouth refused to help, he slowly opened his eyelids but the blinding light shining down on him forced them closed again.

He swung an arm and knocked the lamp that was hanging above his head aside. It swung around on a long cable attached to the ceiling.

He turned onto his side and coughed

harshly. He tried to call out, but his voice was nothing but a raspy bark from being so dry.

He opened his eyes again, slower this time, and took in the room that seemed to sway like a boat on the water in time with the single lamp that swung back and forth.

As far as he could tell he was alone.

He closed his eyes and placed his palms on the bed to push himself up to a sitting position. His head screamed with the change in position and commanded him to lay back down immediately.

He ignored it and waited for the wave of vertigo to subside before he opened his eyes again.

The room around him was small and

empty. Except for the bed he was on, there was nothing else in the small room.

He looked down at the bed and noticed that it was not a bed at all but a table in the center of the room.

Why was he lying on a table?

He swung his feet slowly over the edge of the table and brushed aside the ceiling mounted lamp with one hand right before it smacked him in the side of his head.

He leaned forward out of range of the swinging lamp and carefully hopped off the table. Once on the ground, he saw two chairs sitting under the table, their backs low enough to allow them to be slid fully under and out of sight.

Massaging his temples, he looked around

the sparsely furnished room and spotted the door.

He started for it when the chair in front of him slid out and he felt invisible hands push him down into it.

It caught him by surprise and he found himself sitting in the chair before he even fully registered that the chair had moved on its own.

It was then that he noticed the additional shadows cast on the wall by the still swaying lamp.

The pressure on his shoulders lessened and he was released by the two shadows that had shoved him into the chair.

One of the shadows moved toward the door, opened it, and disappeared from the

room.

With only one shadow in the room, Dylan tried to stand up again, but was forced back down by strong hands.

"Are you going to tell me what this is all about?" he croaked.

His throat was still raw from the potion that had put him to sleep. He hadn't seen what had stabbed into him, but he felt it, and quickly succumbed to the effects of whatever had been injected into his body.

Now that those effects were wearing off, he was feeling a little more brazen. Especially because there was only one other person in the room with him.

Invisible or not, he liked those odds.

Dylan tilted his head to the side and used

the light from the still swaying lamp to judge where his captor's head was in relation to his own. He could see the two shadows moving at slightly different angles as the lamp swung back and forth.

His muscles tensed as he tested his strength by gripping and pulling on the edge of his cloak.

His strength had returned enough.

He watched the shadow standing above him and then glanced at the door.

"Did you hear that?"

He looked back to see the head of the shadow swivel toward the door.

It was now or never.

He jumped up and swung out, catching the invisible man just under the chin with his forearm.

Not the best hit he could have hoped for, but it knocked the man off balance enough for Dylan to reach out with his other hand and grab the man by the hair.

Once he had the man's hair, he twisted his hand until he got his other arm around the man's neck.

He pulled the invisible man in close and tightened his arm against the man's throat.

The only sound in the room was Dylan's grunting as he chocked the man unconscious.

He slowly lowered the invisible body to the floor and let go. Feeling against the man's clothing, he found a pocket.

Inside was a key that became visible once

it was removed from the pocket. He stuck his hand in the pocket again and watched it disappear.

The man's clothing was as invisible as he was. This was exactly what Dylan needed to get away.

He tugged at the man's coat. It wasn't easy removing it without being able to see what he was doing, but Dylan had grown up a thief and was used to robbing people under the cover of darkness as a small child. It didn't take long for him to remove the man's clothing and put it on himself.

He looked down and was pleased to see that every part of his body covered by the man's liberated clothing was now invisible.

He pulled the man's shirt off his sleeping

body and pulled it over his head. He could see through it to walk around without bumping into walls, and hopefully it kept him from being seen at all.

Dylan unlocked the door with the key and opened the door slowly. He peeked out.

The hallway was empty.

This was going to be a piece of cake, he thought right before he was tackled to the ground and held down, his chest compressed under so much weight, he was unable to catch his breath.

The one thing he didn't expect was that, to the invisible people, none of their clothing was invisible to them.

Chapter 15

Josh straightened up and moved closer to Suzy and Andre.

"We aren't alone," he whispered.

"Shh," Suzy said and pointed at Larissa.

Larissa was watching words form on the dirt floor and smiling. She was whispering softly and nodding her head as the words smeared away to make room for more words.

After a few minutes, Larissa looked up at the trio.

"We are amongst friends. Essence said that she has been tasked with helping us on our quest."

"She's going to help us?" Suzy asked.

Larissa nodded.

"She said that she was selected out of everyone in her group to be the one."

Andre took a step forward.

"Did she know about our quest before now?"

"Yes."

"By who?"

Larissa smiled.

"My father. Herobrine."

Josh, Andre, and Suzy looked at each other. Andre looked back at Larissa.

"When did he ask for her help?"

"She said he told her this morning."

"This morning? That's not possible."

Larissa frowned.

"She's not lying to me."

"I didn't say she was lying," replied Andre. "It's just that…"

He looked over at Suzy who sighed and took over to finish what he didn't want to say.

Larissa followed his look and stared at Suzy.

"What?"

Suzy swallowed loudly before beginning.

"Herobrine, your father, we lost him a couple days ago."

"And he came back here to recruit Essence."

Suzy shook her head.

"By lost, I mean he died."

Larissa was shaking her head violently.

"But Essence said…"

Suzy smiled sadly.

"I know what she told you, but we all saw it, we tried to stop it…"

"Stop what? What are you saying?"

"A cave spider took him and we couldn't save him. We tried to save him."

Dust lifted up from the floor as words were swept away quickly and replaced with more words.

They all watched as the letters formed rapidly and then suddenly stopped before the message was complete.

HEROBRINE IS A

Larissa spoke into the empty air.

"Herobrine is a what? What is Herobrine?"

When there was no response, Larissa waved her hand around near the letters.

"Essence? What were you trying to say? Where is my father?"

There was no response.

Larissa kept waving her hand slowly around in front of her, trying to feel for something that wasn't there.

She shot a look at the three of them.

"Help me find her!"

Josh reached out and felt around while walking slowly, like a blind man trying to find his way across an unfamiliar room.

They searched the entire room, but didn't find anyone. Andre held the torch low, casting their shadows high into the air.

"Where are they?" Andre asked to the

room.

Suzy looked at him.

"Where are who?"

"All the shadows."

Josh looked at the walls.

The last time he had paid attention, it was filled with shadows cast by the large crowd of invisible bodies. Now, the walls were brightly lit by the torch in every direction.

Josh spun slowly, gaping at the empty walls around the room.

The only shadows he could see were the four of them.

All the extra shadows that had been in the room before were now gone.

They were alone.

Chapter 16

Dylan was lifted in the air and carried back through the door into the room. He struggled against the many hands that held him tightly as they slammed him onto the table and pulled straps up from around the edges. The straps moved on their own, like snakes made from flat leather, and secured him firmly to the top of the table.

He wriggled and flexed, but the straps refused to budge.

The doorway darkened as someone entered.

Dylan faced the door and saw a man enter the room, casting two shadows on the wall as he walked.

No, that wasn't accurate.

He cast one shadow while the second shadow was made by someone walking in with him.

The man talked quietly to himself, pausing as if he was conducting both sides of the conversation on his own.

The man listened to the silence, then shook his head as he focused his attention on Dylan.

The man smiled as he looked down at Dylan.

"They tell me you invaded their space. Might I ask what it was you were looking for so far underground?"

Dylan's forehead wrinkled in confusion.

"You can hear them?"

"Of course," the man replied. "Now, what were you doing so far from the surface?"

"I don't see how that's any of your business."

The man chuckled.

"You'd be surprised at how much of what goes on around here is my business. They have spared your life because you were rescued by the zombie. But that reprieve is not absolute, and you might want to start talking before they change their minds."

"I was actually escaping from prison with some guy named..."

Dylan paused, trying to remember and then suddenly laughed.

"Actually, I never asked for his name. Did you catch him again too? Maybe you can ask him why we were so far below the surface."

"The man you are talking about escaped when the zombie tried to rescue you. We were not able to capture him again."

"Well, then I don't know what to tell you. He dug the hole that led to my prison cell and I just followed him down it."

The man tilted his head, as if listening to something, then nodded as he faced Dylan.

"Why didn't you stay at the surface? Why did you keep digging?"

"I was trying to get into the castle's vault."

"Why?"

"It has something I'm looking for."

"Were you planning to rob the castle's

vault?"

Dylan attempted to shrug but the leather straps that bound him made the motion challenging.

"Maybe in a past life I would have done that. But not this time."

The man leaned over him.

"What were you looking for?"

Dylan looked away from him.

"I'm sorry, but I swore on my life to keep that a secret."

"Okay," the man continued. "Why was the zombie trying to save your life?"

Dylan turned back to the man.

"Where is she? What have you done with her?"

"I am asking the questions."

"I am done answering," Dylan said and then looked away.

The man pinched Dylan's face and forced Dylan to face him.

"If I answer one of your questions, will you answer one of mine?"

"Okay," Dylan mumbled, his face crunched up in the strong grip of the man's hand. The man released Dylan and took a big breath.

"How do you know the zombie?"

Dylan's eyes smoldered at the memory of the true circumstances surrounding his relationship with Larissa.

"She stole my dragon."

The man's eyebrows raised.

"I see."

Dylan glared at him.

"Now you answer one of mine."

The man nodded. "Okay."

"Do you know where she is?"

"Yes."

"Where is she?"

The man held up a finger.

"Ah, ah, ahh. That is a second question. I believe you have to answer one of mine next."

Dylan tried to get comfortable, but the straps bit into his muscles and held him fast to the table.

The man tapped a finger on his upper lip, studying Dylan for a full minute before speaking again.

"Are you helping the zombie with a

quest?"

"Yes," Dylan replied.

"What is it?"

Dylan smiled.

"That's a second question. I believe it's my turn."

The man smiled back.

"Touché. Ask your question."

"Where is she?"

"You are asking about the zombie?"

"Yes."

"She is safe. Now, what is your quest?"

"You didn't answer my question."

"Yes I did."

"I asked you where she was."

"And I told you she was safe."

"That's not an answer."

"It's the best answer I can give you."

"Then you don't know where she is."

Their eyes burned into each other for a long moment before the man's eyes softened.

"No. I don't know where she is at this moment in time, but I do know she is safe."

"How can you be so sure?"

"Because she is with the Sciamachy. They will keep her safe."

"How do you know?"

"Because they owe me."

"What did you do for them?"

The man's eyes hardened again and got a faraway look, as if he was thinking about something in the past that didn't make him happy. His eyes refocused on Dylan and his expression changed to a calmer demeanor.

"I believe it's my turn to ask a question."

"Ask away."

"What is the nature of your quest?"

Dylan thought back to the non-answers that this man had given him and decided that two could play at that game.

"I am supposed to recover an item."

The man nodded, turned his head, and whispered under his breath.

The door to the room opened and a small wooden box floated into the room.

The man took the box and held it in front of him. He opened the box and lifted out the glowing Crystal Cube that Larissa had lost.

"You mean this?"

Dylan's eyes nearly popped out of his

head. How did this man know what he was looking for?

He looked at the man in shock. He obviously knew more about Dylan than Dylan knew about him. It was time to change that.

The man replaced the cube in the box and it floated back out of the room.

"Your turn."

Dylan knew the next question he would ask. He just wasn't sure he was prepared for the answer.

Dylan cleared his throat.

"What's your name?"

"I thought you would never ask," the man said as he smiled warmly at him.

"My name is Herobrine."

The Adventure Continues...
Season Two - Episode 3
Fellowship of the Block

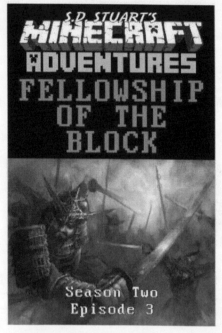

Sign up for Steve's Book Release Bulletin

to be alerted when this book comes out

S.D. Stuart's Minecraft Adventures:

Season Two

War of Darkness

Child of Shadow

Fellowship of the Block

The Dark King

The Vampire's Keep

Core Dungeon

Be the first to know when the next book in the Minecraft Adventures series comes out. Follow the URL below to subscribe to my Book Release Bulletin for free today!

http://bit.ly/BookReleaseBulletin

Jason and the Chrononauts:

Season One

The Chronicle of Stone

The Winter's Sun

The Gateway's Mirror

The Forgotten Oracle

The Prophecy's Touch

The Dawn Legend

Be the first to know when the next book in the Jason and the Chrononauts series comes out. Follow the URL below to subscribe to my Book Release Bulletin for free today!

http://bit.ly/BookReleaseBulletin

S.D. Stuart's Steampunk OZ:

Season One

Forgotten Girl

The Legacy's World

Emerald Shadow

The Future's Destiny

S.D. Stuart's Steampunk OZ:

Season Two

The Dangerous Captive

Missing Legacy

Shadow of History

The Edge of the Hunter

Every book in Season One & Season Two is now at your favorite bookstore! Be sure to begin with Forgotten Girl, the book that started it all.

S.D. Stuart's Minecraft Adventures:

Season One

The Portal

Day of the Creepers

Here Be Dragons

The Dark Temple

Immortal Zombie

Displaced Kingdom

Forgotten Reboot

Wither's Destruction

Every book in Season One is now available at your favorite bookstore! Be sure to begin with Herobrine Rises, the book that started it all.

Other Books by S.D. Stuart

The Wizard of OZ: A Steampunk Adventure

The Scarecrow of OZ: A Steampunk Adventure

Fugue: The Cure

Herobrine Rises: A Minecraft Adventure

S.D. Stuart's Minecraft Adventures Series

Jason and the Chrononauts Series

You can find all of these books at your favorite bookstore today!

Writing as Steve DeWinter

Inherit the Throne

The Warrior's Code

The Red Cell Report (COMING SOON)

Be the first to know about Steve DeWinter's next book, and get your exclusive discount for each hot new release. In fact, receive your first exclusive discounts in the "Welcome" Email.

Follow the URL below to subscribe for free today!

http://bit.ly/BookReleaseBulletin

Made in the USA
San Bernardino, CA
27 June 2014